Letter from the Translators

Dear Readers,

We frequently bring our talk "The Magical Encounter Between Books and Children" to readers' communities, and wherever we are, we try to introduce children to books. When a child has found a friend in the pages of a book, that child is already on the path to academic success.

Professionally, we come from the fields of applied linguistics and education, areas in which we have published extensively and on which we have lectured in universities around the world. Personally, we are both daughters of the imagination and friends of discovery. As children's authors we have published hundreds of books, and because we are bilingual, we love to share the treasures hidden in the books of English- and Spanish-speaking authors, which we had an opportunity to do as consultants on the Green Light Readers/Colección Luz Verde series.

It was a pleasure to select these excellent stories with great illustrations for beginning readers and make them available in Spanish in words as engaging as those used in the originals. For the Spanish-speaking child, it will be significant to have access to authentic texts by recognized authors and illustrators in the United States. For the child learning Spanish, it is essential for the language to be not only correct but inspiring.

The early experiences between children and books are key to their future success. Opening the door of wonder, magic, fun, and knowledge through the printed word is the first step for children in loving the world that reading will bring to their lives. With bilingual books, a universal mind can be fostered at very early ages. That is the world our children will need, and we are helping them to get there.

¡Felicidades!

Alma Flor Ada & F. Isabel Campoy

Rabbit and Turtle Go to School

Conejo y Tortuga van a la escuela

Lucy Floyd

Illustrated by/Ilustrado por

Christopher Denise

Green Light Readers   Colección Luz Verde

sandpiper

Houghton Mifflin Harcourt

Boston   New York

"Let's race to school," said Rabbit.

—Vamos a hacer una carrera hasta
la escuela—dijo Conejo.

"You ride the bus and I'll run.

—Tú vas en el autobús y yo corro.

On your mark, get set, go!"

—Preparados, listos, ¡ya!

Rabbit ran fast.
He went up the mountain.

Conejo corría rápido.
Subió la montaña.

Turtle got on the bus.
The bus left.

Tortuga se subió al autobús.
El autobús se puso en marcha.

Rabbit ran very fast.
He ran down the mountain

Conejo corría muy rápido.
Corrió montaña abajo.

The bus stopped.

El autobús se paró.

Rabbit ran very, very fast.
He was almost there.

Conejo corría muy, muy rápido.
Ya casi llegaba.

The bus stopped again.

El autobús volvió a parar.

Rabbit stopped for a snack.

Conejo se detuvo a tomar algo.

Turtle's bus drove by Rabbit

El autobús de Tortuga pasó frente a Conejo

and on to school.

y llegó a la escuela.

"Let's race tomorrow," said Turtle.
"I'll give you a head start."

—Vamos a hacer una carrera mañana —
dijo Tortuga. —Dejaré que salgas primero.

Draw a Map!

Rabbit and Turtle each went
to school a different way.
How do you go to school?

WHAT YOU'LL NEED

 paper

 crayons or markers

1. Look carefully at the main places you see on your way to school.

2. Notice where each place is.

3. Draw your map.

Share your map with a friend!

¡Dibuja un mapa!

Conejo y Tortuga fueron a la escuela
cada uno por un camino distinto.
¿Cómo vas tú a la escuela?

LO QUE VAS A NECESITAR

 papel

 lápices de colores
o marcadores

1. Fíjate bien en los sitios importantes por los que pasas de camino a la escuela.

2. Fíjate en dónde está cada lugar.

3. Dibuja tu mapa.

¡Comparte tu mapa con un amigo o una amiga!

Meet the Illustrator/Conoce al ilustrador

Christopher Denise likes drawing animals. Before he starts to draw, he looks at pictures of real animals to get ideas. He says, "I know children will like a story even more if the animals are really special."

A Christopher Denise le gusta dibujar animales. Antes de empezar a dibujar observa fotos de animales reales para tomar ideas. Dice: "Sé que a los niños les gustará más una historia si los animales son realmente especiales."

About the translators

F. Isabel Campoy and Alma Flor Ada have written more than a hundred books each, and each has translated many books also. But they enjoy writing and translating books in collaboration. It's great fun!

Sobre las traductoras

F. Isabel Campoy y Alma Flor Ada han escrito más de cien libros cada una, y cada una también ha traducido muchos libros. Pero les encanta cuando pueden escribir o traducir libros entre las dos. ¡Es muy divertido!

Copyright © 2000 by Houghton Mifflin Harcourt Publishing Company
Spanish translation copyright © 2010 by Houghton Mifflin Harcourt Publishing Company

www.hmhco.com

First Green Light Readers/Colección Luz Verde edition 2010

SANDPIPER and the SANDPIPER logo are trademarks of Houghton Mifflin Harcourt Publishing Company.

Green Light Readers and its logo are trademarks of Houghton Mifflin Harcourt Publishing Company, registered in the United States of America and/or other jurisdictions.

Library of Congress Cataloging-in-Publication Data is on file.

ISBN 978-0-547-33897-2
ISBN 978-0-547-33898-9 (pb)

Printed in China
SCP 20 19 18 17 16 15 14 13
4500693284

Ages 4–6
Grades: 1
Guided Reading Level: E
Reading Recovery Level: 8

Green Light Readers
For the reader who's ready to GO!

Five Tips to Help Your Child Become a Great Reader

1. Get involved. Reading aloud to and with your child is just as important as encouraging your child to read independently.

2. Be curious. Ask questions about what your child is reading.

3. Make reading fun. Allow your child to pick books on subjects that interest her or him.

4. Words are everywhere—not just in books. Practice reading signs, packages, and cereal boxes with your child.

5. Set a good example. Make sure your child sees YOU reading.

Why Green Light Readers Is the Best Series for Your New Reader

● Created exclusively for beginning readers by some of the biggest and brightest names in children's books

● Reinforces the reading skills your child is learning in school

● Encourages children to read—and finish—books by themselves

● Offers extra enrichment through fun, age-appropriate activities unique to each story

● Incorporates characteristics of the Reading Recovery® program used by educators

● Developed with Harcourt School Publishers and credentialed educational consultants

Colección Luz Verde
¡Para los lectores que están listos para AVANZAR!

Cinco sugerencias para ayudar a que su niño se vuelva un gran lector

1. Participe. Leerle en voz alta a su niño, o leer junto con él, es tan importante como animar al niño a leer por sí mismo.

2. Exprese interés. Hágale preguntas al niño sobre lo que está leyendo.

3. Haga que la lectura sea divertida. Permítale al niño elegir libros sobre temas que le interesen.

4. Hay palabras en todas partes, no sólo en los libros. Anime a su niño a practicar la lectura leyendo carteles, anuncios e información, como en las cajas de cereales.

5. Dé un buen ejemplo. Asegúrese de que su niño vea que USTED lee.

Por qué esta serie es la mejor para los lectores que comienzan

● Ha sido creada exclusivamente para los niños que empiezan a leer, por algunos de los más brillantes e importantes creadores de libros infantiles.

● Refuerza las habilidades de lectura que su niño está aprendiendo en la escuela.

● Anima a los niños a leer libros de principio a fin, por sí solos.

● Ofrece actividades de enriquecimiento, entretenidas y apropiadas para la edad del lector, creadas para cada cuento.

● Incorpora características del programa Reading Recovery® usado por educadores.

● Ha sido desarrollada por la división escolar de Harcourt y por consultores educativos acreditados.

Look for more bilingual Green Light Readers!
Éstos son otros libros de la serie bilingüe Colección Luz Verde

Daniel's Pet/Daniel y su mascota
Alma Flor Ada/G. Brian Karas

Sometimes/Algunas veces
Keith Baker

The Big, Big Wall/ No puedo bajar
Reginald Howard/Ariane Dewey/ Jose Aruego

Big Brown Bear/El gran oso pardo
David McPhail

Big Pig and Little Pig/Cerdo y Cerdito
David McPhail

What Day Is It?/¿Qué día es hoy?
Alex Moran/Daniel Moreton

Daniel's Mystery Egg/El misterioso huevo de Daniel
Alma Flor Ada/G. Brian Karas

Digger Pig and the Turnip/Marranita Poco Rabo y el nabo
Caron Lee Cohen/Christopher Denise

Tumbleweed Stew/Sopa de matojos
Susan Stevens Crummel/Janet Stevens

Chick That Wouldn't Hatch/El pollito que no quería salir del huevo
Claire Daniel/Lisa Campbell Ernst

Get That Pest!/¡Agarren a ése!
Erin Douglas/Wong Herbert Yee

Catch Me If You Can!/¡A que no me alcanzas!
Bernard Most

Farmer's Market/Día de Mercado
Carmen Parks/Edward Martinez